HIP-HOP ARTISTS

NICKI MINAJ

POP RAP ICON

BY LAURA K. MURRAY

Essential Library
An Imprint of Abdo Publishing
abdobooks.com

ABDOBOOKS.COM

Published by Abdo Publishing, a division of ABDO, PO Box 398166, Minneapolis, Minnesota 55439.

Printed in the United States of America, North Mankato, Minnesota.
102021
012022

THIS BOOK CONTAINS RECYCLED MATERIALS

Cover Photo: Shutterstock Images
Interior Photos: Matt Sayles/AP Images, 4, 38–39; Kathy Hutchins/Shutterstock Images, 6; S. Bukley/Shutterstock Images, 10; Marcin Kadziolka/Shutterstock Images, 13; Shutterstock Images, 14, 16; Richard Shotwell/Invision/AP Images, 19, 89; Mark J. Terrill/AP Images, 22; Shareif Ziyadat/FilmMagic/Getty Images, 24; Chris Pizzello/Invision/AP Images, 26; Jordan Strauss/Invision/AP Images, 29; Charles Sykes/AP Images, 32; Carl Bjorklund/Shutterstock Images, 35; Chris Pizzello/AP Images, 36; Ethan Miller/Getty Images for ABC/Getty Images, 42; Ben Liebenberg/AP Images, 44; John Minchillo/AP Images, 46; Joel Ryan/AP Images, 49; Matt Sayles/Invision/AP Images, 52–53, 60, 62–63; Danny Lawson/AP Images, 54; Manuel Nauta/Sipa USA/AP Images, 57; Donald Traill/Invision/AP Images, 58; Evan Agostini/Invision/AP Images, 66; AF Archive/Alamy, 70–71; Aurore Marechal/PA Images/Alamy, 73; Charles Sykes/Invision/AP Images, 76, 81; Jim Ruymen/UPI/Alamy, 79; Yes Market Media/Shutterstock Images, 84; KGC-146/Star Max/IPx/AP Images, 86; Myra Thompson/Shutterstock Images, 88; Debby Wong/Shutterstock Images, 93; Paras Griffin/Getty Images Entertainment/Getty Images, 96

Editor: Arnold Ringstad
Series Designer: Laura Graphenteen

LIBRARY OF CONGRESS CONTROL NUMBER: 2021941058

PUBLISHER'S CATALOGING-IN-PUBLICATION DATA

Names: Murray, Laura K., author.
Title: Nicki Minaj: pop rap icon / by Laura K. Murray
Other title: pop rap icon
Description: Minneapolis, Minnesota : Abdo Publishing, 2022 | Series: Hip-hop artists | Includes online resources and index.
Identifiers: ISBN 9781532196188 (lib. bdg.) | ISBN 9781098217990 (ebook)
Subjects: LCSH: Minaj, Nicki (Onika Maraj-Petty)--Juvenile literature. | Rap musicians--United States--Biography--Juvenile literature. | Rap (Music)--Juvenile literature. | Lyricists--Biography--Juvenile literature. | Actresses--Biography--Juvenile literature.
Classification: DDC 782.421649--dc23

CONTENTS

Chapter ONE

DROPPING THE SUPER BASS

In March 2010, Nicki Minaj was finishing up recording her first studio album. The 27-year-old rapper had received positive feedback on her previously released mixtapes as well as her appearances on the tracks of other artists. Her quick wit, creative flows, and ability to swerve into varying accents and emotions had gained her a growing following of hip-hop fans. However, she hadn't released a solo album and wasn't yet widely known to mainstream listeners.

Working with rapper Lil Wayne's Young Money record label, Minaj knew there was widespread industry anticipation surrounding her upcoming debut album, which was due to drop in November. The album, *Pink Friday*, would feature several big names, including rap legend Eminem, Minaj's friend and fellow Young Money rapper Drake, pop icon Rihanna, and hip-hop star Kanye

Nicki Minaj was widely known in the hip-hop world in 2010, but she hadn't yet broken through to pop superstardom.

West. The album could be the biggest break of Minaj's career, and she knew she had to deliver. She had never shied away from a challenge, so she kept grinding away to refine the tracks—but it felt as though there were still something missing.

Late one night, Minaj was in Los Angeles, California, when her producer Kane Beatz sent her a sample beat that he and producer JMIKE had created. It was perfect. Minaj loved the pop-influenced, melodic sound, and she decided to get to work immediately. After a quick phone call to rouse songwriter Ester Dean out of bed, Minaj

Songwriter Ester Dean helped Minaj assemble the hit song "Super Bass."

headed to the studio for an all-night session. Dean was also inspired by the beat and quickly pulled together a chorus based on her feelings about her own real-life crush, describing her loud heartbeat as "boom-ba-doom-boom."[1]

Meanwhile, Minaj got to work on the flow. She rapped verses with her signature playfulness, weaving in wordplay and unique vocal inflections. The result was an upbeat, catchy song that blended rap with electronic dance music (EDM) and bubblegum pop elements. Titled "Super Bass," its credited writers were Minaj, Beatz (as Daniel Johnson), and Dean. At the end of the night, Minaj knew they had created something special, but even she may not have predicted the song's massive, genre-busting success.

ESTER DEAN, SONG MACHINE

Songwriter, producer, singer, actress, and frequent Minaj collaborator Esther "Ester" Dean was born in 1986 in Oklahoma. She made her mark writing songs for Minaj, Rihanna, and Katy Perry, including Rihanna's "Rude Boy." She went on to write for Beyoncé, Britney Spears, Drake, Selena Gomez, Kelly Clarkson, Usher, Florence + the Machine, and many others. Her success in churning out chart-topping hits resulted in the nickname the Song Machine. She has also appeared in the *Pitch Perfect* films.

DEFINING A DECADE

The legacy of "Super Bass" was long lasting, with a 2019 *Billboard* article listing the song as a definitive song of the 2010s. Its mix of electronic dance music (EDM), a catchy hook, and rapped verses combined for an up-tempo crossover hit that defied genre boundaries. "At first, we didn't quite know what to think of [Minaj]," said Michael Martin, an executive at the radio and broadcasting company Entercom. "We tried to categorize her. But once a song hits a certain level of familiarity, all the sonic barriers and preconceived notions of who that artist and song is supposed to be come crumbling down. And then it just becomes a smash."[2]

SHOOTING FOR STAR STATUS

The rapper had been using music, humor, and drama as a creative outlet since childhood, when she found refuge from a volatile home life by escaping into her imagination. After growing up in Queens, New York, she got experience in the city's rap scene before being discovered by a record producer through her Myspace social media page. Taking the stage name Nicki Minaj, she developed a hip-hop persona that included an ever-growing array of alter egos that she could slip into as easily as her wild, rainbow-colored outfits and wigs.

As Minaj completed *Pink Friday* in 2010, she had to wonder how the hip-hop world and radio listeners would respond to a female rapper. Historically, only a handful of female rappers had found major success. Music journalists from NPR and elsewhere asserted that, in an unspoken rule, the industry unfairly did not allow for more than one or two successful female rappers at a time. According to journalist Nick Soulsby, beginning around the year 2000, women in hip-hop had been mainly relegated to the role of sexualized objects rather than empowered individuals and artists. When hip-hop enthusiasts debated which rapper should hold the title of the greatest of all time, female rappers were often excluded completely from consideration.

Minaj hadn't let any of that diminish her confidence. In October

ALTER EGOS

Throughout Minaj's career, she has developed a wide variety of personae, or alter egos. Each came with its own eccentricities, rap style, and fashion sense. Minaj's alter egos included Harajuku Barbie (shortened to "Barbie" or "HB"), Roman Zolanski, Martha Zolanski, Chun-Li, and others. Alter egos have been commonplace in hip-hop for years. For instance, Makaveli was the alter ego of 1990s rap icon Tupac Shakur. Slim Shady is the sinister alter ego of rapper Eminem—real name Marshall Mathers—who rose to prominence in the early 2000s. Wolf Haley is an alter ego of Tyler, The Creator—real name Tyler Okonma—who became popular in the 2010s. Some rappers use alter egos to express different traits or messages that don't otherwise align with their public identities. Some release entire albums from the alter ego's point of view. Often an alter ego allows a rapper an outlet to be weirder or more menacing, chaotic, or surreal.

Unconventional hairstyles and fashions have become key parts of Minaj's image.

2010, a month before *Pink Friday*'s release, Minaj appeared on the track "Monster" from Kanye West's acclaimed album *My Beautiful Dark Twisted Fantasy*. Her verse didn't just create a buzz—it created a frenzy of interest, with fans, critics, and fellow artists singling her out among the song's other featured players, who included New York rap royalty Jay-Z, rapper Rick Ross, indie-folk artist Justin Vernon, and West himself. The track seemed to cement Minaj's status as the real deal, and it proved she wasn't intimidated to go head-to-head with seasoned rappers.

THE REIGNING QUEEN OF RAP

In November 2010, Minaj's *Pink Friday* album was released, debuting at Number 2 on the *Billboard* 200 and receiving overall positive reviews from critics. However, it wasn't until the following April that Minaj's status truly skyrocketed with the release of "Super Bass" as the album's fifth single. The track hit Number 3 on the *Billboard* Top 100, making it the highest-charting song

"The lack of female rappers has in some ways made it easier to come up because now there's an open lane for me. I salute the female rappers who came before me, but it's my time now."[3]

–Nicki Minaj, 2009

by a solo female rapper in nearly a decade. The last female rapper to hold one of the top spots was Missy Elliott with her hit "Work It," which peaked at Number 2 in 2002.

Listeners couldn't get enough of the catchy beat and Minaj's explosive delivery. "Who else so casually unleashes their personality onto an audience like this?" asked *Spin*'s Brandon Soderberg.[4] *Billboard*'s Dan Weiss labeled it "one of the most blissful escapes the genre has ever spawned."[5] Major stars from Taylor Swift to Selena Gomez publicly gushed about "Super Bass." Within two years, the Recording Industry Association of America (RIAA) would certify the track as eight times platinum, announcing that it had sold eight million copies.

MISSY ELLIOTT

Born Melissa Arnette Elliott in 1971, four-time Grammy-winning rapper, singer, producer, and songwriter Missy Elliott grew up in Virginia. After an abusive childhood, she turned to music and eventually found success writing and performing hip-hop. She followed her acclaimed 1997 debut album, *Supa Dupa Fly*, with a string of successful albums into the mid-2000s. Her best-known hits include "Work It," "Get Ur Freak On," "Lose Control," and "Gossip Folks." With more than 30 million records sold, Elliott is reportedly the top-selling female rapper in history. Many credit her as being a feminist pioneer in the hip-hop industry. According to Kat George in *Dazed* magazine, "If you love Nicki and Beyoncé, it's important to remember the artist who paved the way."[6]

Missy Elliott is among the early female rappers who set the stage for later stars like Minaj.

However, some in the hip-hop industry criticized Minaj for selling out her rap roots to appeal to a wider, commercial audience with a pop crossover. That criticism would continue to plague Minaj throughout the years as she often straddled the line between pop and rap. Meanwhile, other critics accused her of being too sexual, too aggressive, or too dramatic.

Minaj didn't let the critics or doubters bring her down. Instead, she spit even more fire into her lyrics.

Minaj's career has been marked by originality, creativity, and an eye toward superstardom.

After a troubled childhood filled with violence and fear, she was no stranger to adversity. In laying down tracks, she incorporated sharp retorts and comedic comebacks, pointing out the double standard that female rappers were held to, unabashedly highlighting her own prowess, and finding power in turning stereotypes on their heads.

Minaj's visions of reigning supreme as the Queen of Rap seemed to be taking shape, with music critics and media outlets such as *USA Today*, NPR, Yahoo, *Billboard*, and others commonly using that nickname to describe her. As "Super Bass" blew up, Minaj was seeking more than success. She was seeking icon status. She continued pushing her way to the top, looking to prove that she could be not only the Queen of Rap but also a contender for the greatest of all time.

"Nicki Minaj is a real space oddity. Rap has never seen a mainstream rising star this eccentric and brave."[7]

—Caryn Ganz, Out.com

Chapter Two

FROM TRINIDAD TO NEW YORK

Nicki Minaj was born Onika Tanya Maraj on December 8, 1982, in the southern Caribbean country of Trinidad and Tobago. She lived in the Saint James district of the capital city, Port of Spain. Her mother, Carol, worked as an accounting clerk, while her father, Robert, was a financial executive. Onika was the second of the family's four children. Her siblings include her older brother, Jelani; younger brother, Micaiah; and younger sister, Ming. Both Carol and Robert were gospel singers, and Onika grew up singing along to recordings of Diana Ross and her mother's other favorite artists.

Onika had a difficult childhood. Her father was abusive and addicted to drugs. In the late 1980s, he tried to burn down the family's home with Onika's mother inside. When Onika was young, she lived temporarily with her grandmother while Carol moved to New York

Onika spent her early childhood in Port of Spain, Trinidad and Tobago.

to attend school. Robert soon joined Carol in the United States. When Onika was five years old, she and Jelani joined their parents in the New York City borough of Queens. Onika spent the rest of her childhood there. She later stated that she entered the United States as an undocumented immigrant.

Robert's violent and unpredictable behaviors took a toll on the family. "When you have a father who is stealing your furniture and selling it so that he can buy crack [cocaine], you suffer," she later told *Vibe* magazine. "You come home from school and your couch is gone."[1] She recalled that

> **"These amazing reggae artists influenced me more than I think people realize. It's always there on the album—I always at one point on an album have to represent for my island people."[2]**
>
> *—Nicki Minaj*

CAROL MARAJ

Minaj's mother, Carol, has been involved in various creative and charitable efforts. In 2012, she established the Carol Maraj Foundation with the goal to empower women and focus on domestic violence. In 2021, she released a book about her experiences with abuse titled *Leaving My Pain*. Over the years, Maraj has released several of her own gospel singles, including "God's Been Good" and "What Makes You." In 2014, Maraj said that her daughter was the first person she played her new songs for.

Later in life, Carol sometimes accompanied her famous daughter to music industry events.

throughout her childhood and early teenage years, the family was afraid Robert would kill Carol. As a young girl, Onika prayed that she would become rich to be able to take care of her mother.

Onika's volatile family situation caused difficulties in her school life. She later told *Teen Vogue*, "Every time my parents fought, my mother would have us move and I would have to go to a new school, which meant I'd have to face the task of making new friends. I dreaded it."[3] As a result, Onika developed a thick skin and armed herself with a strong attitude and self-confidence. Robert and Carol eventually separated.

A GREAT ESCAPE

Growing up, Onika played softball and went to church with her family. A natural performer, she used her imagination to escape the difficulties of her home life. She enjoyed acting and making up stories. "Fantasy was my reality," she later said.[4] By age 12, she called herself "Cookie" while writing her first rap: "Cookie's the name, chocolate chip is the flavor/Suck up my style like a cherry Life Saver."[5] She recalled that her larger-than-life confidence made her a target for bullying. "I let people know I wasn't going to be pushed around," she said.[6] She often relied on her older brother for backup if there was a fight. Soon she began using humor and a quick wit to deflect negativity.

> **"When I was growing up I thought I'd be a famous actress. Acting came very natural to me. I didn't imagine all this music stuff happening."[7]**
>
> *—Nicki Minaj*

Things took a turn for the better when Onika entered high school. Her flair for performance landed her a spot at the well-known Fiorello H. LaGuardia High School of Music & Art and Performing Arts in Manhattan, where she studied drama and honed her singing talent. "It was the first time I felt like I really fit in," she remembered. "Everyone there was creative. For once, I didn't feel like there was something weird about me."[8] Onika freestyle rapped for fun, initially to make other students laugh. She became known for bursting into verse in the cafeteria.

LaGuardia High School

Minaj's performing arts high school, LaGuardia, is notable for its many famous graduates that span the fields of acting, music, dance, fashion, and other arts. Graduates include Awkwafina, Jennifer Aniston, Corbin Bleu, Liza Minnelli, Al Pacino, Sarah Paulson, and Wesley Snipes. Named for a former New York City mayor, the school was the inspiration behind the 1980 dance movie *Fame*, which follows the stories of students attending the school.

Around this time, Onika began creating different personae for herself as another creative outlet, often slipping into different voices and accents. One alter ego was called "Cookie"—a reference to her first rap and her drama teachers' nickname for her in school. It was also the name

Salt-N-Pepa were among Onika's musical inspirations in the mid-1990s.

of a friend's older sister she admired. As her interest in rap grew, Onika dreamed of meeting her rap idol, Jay-Z. She was a fan of female rappers Salt-N-Pepa, Lil' Kim, and Foxy Brown, as well as male rappers LL Cool J and DMX.

DISCOVERED THROUGH MYSPACE

Upon graduating high school in 2000, Onika auditioned for acting jobs but didn't have success in finding roles.

Meanwhile, she worked during the day at short-lived waitressing jobs. She also did backup singing for local rappers. Soon she started writing her own material, scribbling down raps on her waitressing notepad. It occurred to her that she might be able to turn rapping into a career. For a short time, she was part of a Brooklyn-based rap group called the Hoodstars before deciding to focus on a solo career. "Eventually, I started believing my own hype and being a businesswoman," she later recalled. "I thought, why not take it all the way and put some money in my pocket from it?"[9]

Onika didn't waste any time getting to work. She created a page on the social media platform Myspace to gain exposure. She began trying to contact industry insiders directly, with the help of her then manager, Debra Antney, CEO of Mizay Entertainment and an industry titan behind

NICKI AT RED LOBSTER

According to Minaj, she got fired from several waitressing jobs for having a bad attitude or being rude to customers. In 2019, she talked about her experiences with *The Tonight Show* host Jimmy Fallon as they dined out at a New York City Red Lobster restaurant. Minaj claimed that in one case, she followed customers to their car after they didn't tip her, and she was fired immediately. As part of the late-night show's comedic segment, Minaj and Fallon donned uniforms and tried their hand at serving customers for the cameras.

several big names in hip-hop. Onika's Myspace page caught the eye of Big Fendi, the CEO of Brooklyn-based independent record label Dirty Money Entertainment. In 2007, Big Fendi signed her to a short-term recording

Debra Antney has worked with artists such as Gucci Mane and Waka Flocka Flame, her son.

contract. He suggested that she take the stage name Nicki Minaj rather than Nicki Maraj, believing the new name was a better fit.

Dirty Money distributed street DVDs that included rapper interviews and freestyle rapping. In 2007, Minaj appeared on Dirty Money's DVD "The Come Up: Volume 11 (Carter Edition)." Her performance caught the attention of Lil Wayne, a best-selling rapper who had recently founded his own record label, Young Money Entertainment. Lil Wayne asked Minaj to collaborate with Young Money. The opportunity would prove to be a career changer for Minaj.

LIL WAYNE

Born Dwayne Michael Carter Jr. in Louisiana in 1982, Minaj's mentor Lil Wayne has had tremendous industry success and ranks among the best-selling rappers of all time. He was signed at age 12 by rapper Birdman to Cash Money Records. He later became CEO of his own record label, Young Money Entertainment. In the late 1990s, he was part of the popular southern rap group the Hot Boys. He released his first solo album in 1999, *Tha Block Is Hot*. His many awards include five Grammys. The media has widely covered his criminal issues, as he was convicted on weapons charges in 2010. After pleading guilty to a federal weapons charge in late 2020, he was pardoned by outgoing US president Donald Trump.

Chapter THREE

OF MONSTERS AND MIXTAPES

In April 2007, Minaj released a mixtape under the Dirty Money label called *Playtime Is Over*. The following April, she released a mixtape called *Sucka Free*. She quickly gained a dedicated fan base, and she stayed active on social media sites such as Twitter and Myspace, steadily increasing awareness. Minaj was also receiving early support within the rap world. Lil Wayne proved to be a valuable mentor, helping her navigate the industry. In addition to Lil Wayne, other rappers, such as Gucci Mane and Lil' Kim, made guest appearances on her mixtapes.

During this time, Minaj introduced one of her best-known and longest-lasting alter egos. Harajuku Barbie—called simply "Barbie" or "HB" for short—was a soft-spoken, doll-like figure obsessed with the color pink. According to Minaj, the character was inspired by the Harajuku district of Tokyo, Japan. "The way they dress is

Minaj has collaborated with Lil Wayne throughout her career.

the way I am on the inside. Free spirited, girls that just wanna have fun. . . . That's how I feel and that's what my music is going to feel like, when I do my album," she said.[1] Minaj's growing legion of fans began calling themselves "Barbies," shortened to "Barbz." They embraced Minaj's unabashed confidence, fierce rapping skills, and signature style of brightly colored clothes and wigs.

A BARBIE FOR CHARITY

Minaj's signature Barbie look led to a collaboration with the famous doll's brand. In 2011, Mattel created a Nicki Minaj Barbie doll. The one-of-a-kind doll was put up for auction to benefit the nonprofit organization Project Angel Food, which provides food for people affected by HIV and AIDS.

FIRST LADY OF YOUNG MONEY

In August 2009, Minaj became the first female artist signed to Lil Wayne's Young Money Entertainment label. "To say I'm excited would be an understatement," she said. "It's validation. It's proof. It's empowerment. I represent every little girl in a hood near you. . . . You've given girls all around the world the permission to change the face of female rap."[2] Her career quickly took off as she became known as the "Queen Bee" or "First Lady" in Young Money's talented crew of up-and-comers. This group performed together and hit the road as part of the America's Most Wanted Music Festival tour. Nicknamed the YMCMB ("Young Money Cash Money Billionaires"), the crew also included Canadian actor and rapper Drake, who had recently had a run of successful mixtapes. Minaj and Drake's relationship would be a

> "Nicki Minaj often describes herself as a Barbie doll. But don't let the cute moniker fool you. Minaj's aggressive flow and fearless wordplay have pegged her as a rising star within Lil Wayne's Young Money crew."[3]
>
> —*Jason S. Lipshutz*, Billboard

Lil Wayne's Young Money Entertainment has released hit albums from numerous major artists.

popular topic among fans and media in the coming years as people speculated on their romantic status.

NICKI AND DRAKE

Over the years, Minaj and Drake fueled rumors over the nature of their relationship while denying they were romantically involved. In 2010, they tweeted they were married, and Drake appeared in the music video for Minaj's "Moment 4 Life," in which they rapped about getting married. The two also have had several public fallings-out but have remained friends and musical collaborators since their Young Money days.

Minaj found increased success with the release of her 2009 mixtape *Beam Me Up Scotty*. The mixtape cemented her fan base and brought her to the attention of more listeners. For the first time, her songs entered the *Billboard* charts, with "I Get Crazy" charting on Hot Rap Songs and Hot R&B/Hot Hip-Hop Songs. Though Minaj boasted a lineup of talented collaborators, including Drake, Busta Rhymes, and Gucci Mane, critics praised her for not being overshadowed.

STAR-STUDDED COLLABS

Minaj's popularity continued to rise in 2010 as she received the approval of industry insiders—including Jay-Z. On Jay-Z's recommendation, singer Robin Thicke featured Minaj on one of his tracks, which led to her performing on

The Late Show with David Letterman. Minaj was floored that her longtime idol was a fan of her music. "Jay-Z is a person in hip-hop that you almost don't think he exists until you meet him," Minaj told MTV News. "I didn't think he knew who I was, let alone recommend me for something."[4]

Minaj's celebrity collaborations continued, with singles including "Lil Freak" with Usher, "Bottoms Up" with Trey Songz, and "Letting Go (Dutty Love)" with Sean Kingston. Minaj's alter egos were out in full force, with "Bottoms Up" featuring Barbie and Roman Zolanski, another of Minaj's most used alter egos. According to Minaj, Roman was a gay male character who was more aggressive and outspoken than her usual personality. *Billboard* praised Minaj's "16-bar,

YOUNG MONEY ROCKS MSG

Minaj lived out a dream in early 2010 when she and fellow Young Money crew members performed a last-minute guest spot at New York City's Madison Square Garden during Jay-Z's *Blueprint 3* tour. Being a New York rapper, Minaj saw it as a major milestone to be not only a performer at the famed venue but also a rare female artist who was accepted in the hip-hop industry. "This means the world to me—to be there with Jay-Z, Lil Wayne, Young Jeezy, and Drake," she said. "It was the stuff that dreams are made of for a girl. Girls aren't usually in those unique little circles."[5]

Minaj signed autographs for fans after the taping of *The Late Show with David Letterman*.

off-the-wall performance . . . [that] leaves the listeners blissfully whiplashed."[6]

In addition to teaming up with well-known rappers, Minaj featured on songs with global pop stars Christina Aguilera and Mariah Carey. One of her most successful tracks of 2010 was Ludacris's "My Chick Bad," which earned Minaj her first Grammy nomination when it was given a nod for Best Rap Performance by a Duo or Group. By the fall of 2010, Minaj had made more than 30 of what the *New Yorker*'s Lizzy Goodman called "scene-stealing" guest appearances on big-name songs and videos. Her Twitter following had ticked up to more than 1.5 million.[7]

Minaj was also racking up awards, receiving Best Female Hip-Hop Artist at the 2010 BET Awards. She would go on to win the award each year through 2016. She received her first MTV Video Music Awards (VMA) nomination for Best New Artist. Meanwhile, she was releasing the first singles from her upcoming album. Her single "Your Love" hit Number 1 on the *Billboard* Rap Songs chart,

HASHTAG RAP

Despite its Grammy nomination, not everyone was a fan of "My Chick Bad." In the *Village Voice*, Christopher Weingarten named the track among the 20 worst of the year. He criticized Ludacris for being the worst example of the newly popular "hashtag rap," which involved saying a line, pausing, and finishing with a pun. For instance, Ludacris raps, "Comin' down the street like a parade—Macy's!" Kanye West claimed to have invented hashtag rap, but older usages exist. Weingarten cited examples of Minaj, Drake, and others using this flow. "If this continues in 2011, rap is going to sound like listening to a bad round of Pictionary," he wrote.[8]

making her the first solo female rapper to hold the top spot since Missy Elliott in 2002.

MONSTER UNLEASHED

The track that catapulted 27-year-old Minaj to new heights in the eyes of peers, critics, fans, and mainstream listeners alike was Kanye West's "Monster," on which she delivered a 32-bar verse. Released in September 2010, the song featured several MCs rapping in successive verses. In addition to Minaj and West, "Monster" featured Jay-Z, rapper Rick Ross, and folk artist Justin Vernon of Bon Iver.

Minaj entered the track like a force of nature, spitting out wordplay and accents. She made pop-culture references that ranged from horror movies to fashion designers, and she gave shout-outs to the Young Money crew and her Barbz. She jumped between her Barbie and Roman Zolanski alter egos, showing she wasn't intimidated to step up to the mic with rap legends.

As it turned out, West almost cut the song from the album so it wouldn't upstage the rest of the release. Minaj later revealed that she had to convince him to keep the track. In the end, West relented, although he was right in predicting that hers would be the standout verse that left reverberations across the hip-hop universe. "All that

A 2010 collaboration with Kanye West gave Minaj an opportunity to showcase her impressive rapping talent.

other stuff fades into the background when Nicki Minaj shows up," wrote Tom Breihan of Pitchfork.[9] Josh Glicksman of *Billboard* announced, "Minaj is both the rookie of the year and the league's most valuable player."[10]

> **"She reminds me of myself the way she says whatever she wants however she wants on record. . . . Nicki makes rapping fun again."[11]**
>
> ***–Missy Elliott***

Chapter FOUR

RAP QUEEN OR POP PRINCESS?

In 2010, Minaj had the most songs on the *Billboard* charts in a single year of any female artist in history, with eight. However, she still had her work cut out for her in convincing people to take her talent seriously. For all the buzz surrounding Minaj, she had still not released an official solo album. Because most of the charting songs featured Minaj as a guest, some people felt she still had a lot to prove. The pressure got more intense when her first solo single, "Massive Attack," had a disappointing performance and was pulled from her upcoming album.

Minaj's first studio album, *Pink Friday*, was released in November 2010. With Minaj sitting in a doll-like pose on the pink cover, it debuted at Number 2 on the *Billboard* 200. It sold more than 375,000 copies within its first week. *Pink Friday* became the first solo album by a woman rapper to go platinum in seven years, since

Minaj made a pink-haired appearance at the MTV Video Music Awards in September 2010, just a few months ahead of the release of *Pink Friday*.

A live performance in December 2010 showed off yet another new hairstyle for Minaj.

Lil' Kim's *La Bella Mafia* hit that milestone in 2003. Minaj's album eventually went triple platinum.

The album featured a mixture of pop and rap elements. Some tracks had clear pop sensibilities, such as "Your Love," "Check It Out," and "Save Me." On others, Minaj mixed her rap verses with catchy pop hooks, including "Moment 4 Life," which featured Drake, and "Right Thru Me." A few tracks were pure rap, such as the much-talked-about "Roman's Revenge," which featured Eminem. The song was widely seen as a diss track directed at rapper Lil' Kim, with Minaj rapping that she was taking Lil' Kim's place as queen. The track also introduced another alter ego: Martha Zolanski, Roman's mother. In a *Billboard* cover story, Mariel Concepcion praised Minaj's easy character leaps, writing, "In a matter of bars, Minaj switches effortlessly from the toned-down Onika to the

energetic Nicki and then to her tempestuous alter ego, Roman Zolanski."[1]

ROMAN'S REVENGE

In "Roman's Revenge," Minaj and Eminem rapped as their alter egos Roman Zolanski and Slim Shady, respectively, which were known for being angrier and more aggressive than the rappers' normal personae. Some listeners were critical of the Slim Shady verses that contained harsh language used against women and gay people. Still, Minaj's delivery got positive marks. MTV.com stated that the song "arguably quieted any doubts about [Minaj's] status as [a] full-fledged rap force." Minaj thought the track was the most fun on the album, saying, "It gave me life."[2] "Roman's Revenge" reached Number 56 on the *Billboard* charts.

THINKING PINK

Despite the success of *Pink Friday*, it wasn't until early 2011 that Minaj found herself becoming a household name. In January, singer Selena Gomez put a cover of "Super Bass" on her YouTube channel. In February, pop superstar Taylor Swift was being interviewed on a Nashville radio station when she was asked to request a song. She chose "Super Bass," even rapping part of it. She later tweeted about the song to her legion of followers. That month, the *Pink Friday* album hit Number 1 on the *Billboard* 200.

When "Super Bass" was released as *Pink Friday*'s fifth single in April 2011, it quickly shot to the top of the charts.

In May, the "Super Bass" official music video premiered online. With its colorful hues and bubblegum vibes matching the song's poppy tone, the video quickly racked up millions of views. As she accepted the 2011 *Billboard* Rising Star Award, Minaj thanked Swift for introducing her music to new listeners.

FASHION MUSE

In January 2011, Minaj appeared on *Saturday Night Live* as the musical guest. More celebrity collaborations followed, including hit tracks with Drake, rapper Big Sean, and French DJ David Guetta. Minaj gained more exposure when she joined pop star Britney Spears's Femme Fatale tour. Spears also featured Minaj and singer Kesha on a remix of her track "Till the World Ends." The remix peaked at Number 3 on *Billboard*'s Hot

THE "SB" CONNECTION?

As "Super Bass" took off, many fans speculated on the significance of its initials, which matched the name of Minaj's longtime boyfriend, rapper Safaree "SB" Samuels. Some sources reported the two were secretly engaged or married. Listeners wondered if the first initials of "Super Bass" were an intentional reference to SB the person. Samuels appeared at the end of the song's music video. The two reportedly dated for more than a decade before breaking up in 2014.

Minaj performed with Britney Spears at the 2011 Billboard Music Awards.

100 chart and surpassed two million downloads within a few months.

Minaj's fans continued to embrace not only her music but also her confidence and ever-changing personae. As Minaj built her brand, she was attracting the attention of the fashion world, becoming known as something of a style trendsetter. First, there was the hair. Minaj often wore colorful, avant-garde wigs, which ranged from blunt-cut green bobs and swirled platinum updos to teased pink curls and leopard-print beehives. Minaj employed a full-time wigmaker to create her elaborate styles.

Next, there was the outrageous wardrobe. With Minaj posing for covers in *Elle*, *Cosmopolitan*, and *W* magazines, an article in the *New York Times* announced that "few in 2011 could take their eyes off . . . the Technicolor Barbie with the big voice and elastic smile."[3] Minaj's multicolored outfits created a buzz at awards shows, performances, and red-carpet events as photographers waited to see what wild ensemble she would wear next. Fashion designers took notice and scrambled to work with her. Minaj also launched a nail polish line with the company OPI and had cosmetics deals with MAC Viva Glam.

"Color makes me happy. It really excites me. I am a very visual person and when I look in the mirror, and I see green or I see pink, it does something to my attitude. It makes me feel positive."[4]

–Nicki Minaj

BIG SPOTLIGHTS

In February 2012, Minaj performed in the Super Bowl XLVI halftime show in Indianapolis, Indiana, as a guest of headliner Madonna. Along with rapper M.I.A., Minaj was featured in Madonna's song "Give Me All Your Luvin." For Minaj, seeing Madonna's work ethic and expectations for perfection was a career-changing experience. "When I saw that, it inspired me so much, the same way [Lil] Wayne inspired me to start really becoming a beast as a rapper," she told radio interviewer Ryan Seacrest. "The Madonna situation inspired me to give it my all and put that work in."[5]

Minaj joined Madonna, *center*, and M.I.A., *right*, for a performance on one of the world's largest stages, the Super Bowl halftime show, in 2012.

At the 54th Grammy Awards, Minaj earned nominations for Best New Artist, Best Rap Album (*Pink Friday*), Best Rap Performance ("Moment 4 Life"), and Album of the Year (as a featured artist on Rihanna's *Loud*). During the Grammys, Minaj made headlines with not only her outfit but also a controversial live performance of her new single "Roman Holiday." It featured a mock exorcism of her Roman Zolanski alter ego, complete with gyrating dancers dressed as religious figures.

Social media lit up in response to the performance. While some fans loved it, the Catholic League condemned it, and some critics thought Minaj was simply courting controversy. For her part, Minaj said she had stayed true to her vision for the character of fighting back against the expectation to conform. According to Minaj, the performance showed that people fear Roman for his out-of-the-box personality, wanting him to blend in with the crowd. "Not only is he amazing and . . . confident, but he's never gonna change."[6]

LOOK IT UP

As Minaj became known for making up her own words and phrases, she coined the term "Nictionary" for her unique vocabulary. In 2011, she released her own app in which users could look up explanations for her slang and lyrics.

Chapter FIVE

STARSHIPS ASCENDING

On February 14, 2012, Minaj appeared on Ryan Seacrest's radio show to premiere "Starships," the new single off her upcoming album. Awash in Euro-pop beats, the track featured a catchy chorus. Music critics gave "Starships" overall positive reviews, with *Billboard* calling it her "most radio-friendly single to date."[1] In Digital Spy, reviewer Robert Copsey remarked that rather than coming across as a generic pop song, "Starships" was refreshing because of Minaj's one-of-a-kind eccentricities. The track eventually went six times platinum, and its music video won Best Female Video at the 2012 MTV VMAs.

In April 2012, the 29-year-old Minaj released her second solo album, *Pink Friday: Roman Reloaded*. Named for her alter ego Roman Zolanski, *Roman Reloaded* debuted at Number 1 on the *Billboard* 200. Featured artists included Chris Brown, 2 Chainz, Rick Ross, Nas,

In 2012, Minaj's latest music and show business ventures pushed her career to new heights.

Drake, and Lil Wayne. Its tracks "Pound the Alarm" and "Va Va Voom" cracked the top 25 of the *Billboard* Hot 100. The album's release came on the heels of a *New York Times* article in which writer Jon Caramanica called Minaj "the most influential female rapper of all time."[2]

POP BY PERCENTAGES

Ben Carter of the website CentralSauce called *Pink Friday: Roman Reloaded* "one of the most unique albums in hip-hop history" for its nearly half-and-half division of pop and rap tracks.[4] Analyzing the styles of each song, he described the album's first seven tracks as nearly entirely rap. Next were five songs—including "Starships"—that were a blend of rap and pop. The following six songs were completely pop, while the album concluded with an entirely rap track. Drake displayed a similar pattern on his 2018 album *Scorpion*, on which he rapped in the first half and sang in the second.

Critics were divided about the album, with some again questioning Minaj's mix of genres, as the album was roughly half pop and half rap. Some journalists were unimpressed with Minaj's pop offerings, saying that she wasn't as skilled or exciting when performing pop numbers. In a scathing review, *Slant*'s Matthew Cole called Minaj's multiple personalities "gimmicks" and the pop numbers "generic."[3] However, others praised Minaj's versatility and different styles and sounds. Giving the album four out of five stars, *Rolling Stone*'s Jody

Rosen remarked that Minaj "doesn't just straddle pop categories, she dumps them in a [blender], whips them to a frothy puree, then trains a guided missile at the whole mess."[5] Minaj's fan base continued to grow, and she followed the album with a concert tour that spanned several continents.

CHECKING OUT OF SUMMER JAM

In June 2012, Minaj was slated to take the stage at the annual Summer Jam festival at New Jersey's Met Life

Minaj performed at a music festival in London in June 2012.

Stadium. The event was hosted by New York hip-hop radio station Hot 97. Mere hours before she was due onstage, Minaj backed out of the performance. Peter Rosenberg, a DJ for the station, had criticized Minaj on air, accusing her of lacking authenticity and blasting her recent track "Starships." He had been a longtime critic of Minaj, previously calling her a sellout for her pop stylings.

Minaj's mentor did not take kindly to the insults. As Summer Jam began, Lil Wayne tweeted that the Young Money crew would not be performing. Minaj soon tweeted a confirmation herself, writing that she would not go against her boss's direction. She added, "We won't b disrespected."[6] Lil Wayne also pulled other Young Money performers, including DJ Khaled, from the festival lineup.

BIGGER DISCUSSIONS

The Hot 97 Summer Jam rift led to larger conversations about the evolution of hip-hop. In the *New York Times*, Jon Caramanica pointed out that Minaj was one of only two featured female artists set to perform that day, the other being Harlem rapper Azealia Banks. He wrote that keeping the definition of hip-hop too narrow would prevent the genre from growing. "To reject 'Starships' is to reject the idea of hip-hop as a big tent with room for multiple ideas and micromovements and polarities," he wrote. "That creates the sort of boundary designed to discourage outsiders, innovation, and difference."[7]

AN AMERICAN IDOL

In 2012, Minaj joined the judging panel on the twelfth season of the popular reality singing competition *American Idol*. She appeared with longtime judge and record producer Randy Jackson, as well as fellow newcomer judges Mariah Carey and country music star Keith Urban. Her salary was a reported $12 million.

Minaj proved to be divisive among the show's viewers. Some were turned off by her brazen critiques and unpredictable antics that included walking off set or talking in a British accent. Others appreciated her for the same reasons, finding her comedic delivery entertaining. "Put bluntly, Nicki makes *Idol* worth watching again," said *Today*'s Craig Berman.[8]

"I used to read the bad things people said about me. Then I asked myself, 'Why am I reading that when I have millions of people saying great things?' You cannot give negativity power."[9]

—*Nicki Minaj*, Teen Vogue

However, widely publicized hostility between Minaj and Carey soon overshadowed the show's contestants. While media and tabloid coverage fixated on the relationship between the two judges, some questioned

Minaj had a short tenure as a judge on the hit show *American Idol.*

how much of the feud was exaggerated to get better ratings. *Rolling Stone* pointed out "the readiness of outlets like TMZ to pounce on even the slightest hint of catfight tension between the judging panel's female half."[10] The much-reported drama did not lift the show's slumping ratings. Neither Minaj nor Carey returned for another season. On Twitter, Minaj declared she would be focusing on her music.

Meanwhile, Minaj continued embarking on new ventures. In July 2012, she got into feature films, voicing the character of a woolly mammoth named Steffie in *Ice*

Age 4: Continental Drift. In 2013, she launched a clothing line with Kmart. Whether in music or elsewhere, Minaj was willing to put in the work, and it appeared to be paying off as she saw her star status continue to climb.

RETHINKING ACTING

Although Minaj had dreamed of becoming an actor growing up, she told BET in 2018 that acting no longer held the same appeal. She cited the tedium of being on set and doing press tours. "I realized that maybe it's not in me like rap is in me," she said. "With rap, it's different, no matter how long it takes I'm willing to do it. I just don't have that same passion [for acting]."[11]

MAKING A PINKPRINT

Chapter SIX

In 2014, Minaj continued her prolific streak as a featured artist. She guested with Beyoncé on "Flawless" and with Jessie J and Ariana Grande on the smash hit "Bang Bang." She also hosted the MTV Europe Music Awards in Scotland. But it was "Anaconda," the second single off her upcoming album *The Pinkprint*, that got everybody talking.

Released in August 2014, "Anaconda" was a rap track that sampled the 1992 hit song "Baby Got Back" by Sir Mix-A-Lot, which was known for its sexually suggestive lyrics. "Anaconda" hit Number 2 on the *Billboard* Hot 100 and peaked at Number 1 on the Hot Rap chart. Many critics reviewed the song positively, praising it as an empowering and comedic take on the original song. The track later received a Grammy nomination for Best Rap Song. However, others accused it of being a bad influence on young girls, with AJ Delgado of *National Review* stating,

Minaj made a dramatic entrance at the 2014 MTV Europe Music Awards.

"The music industry is laughing all the way to the bank while teaching women to devalue themselves—at what point will we say it is going too far?"[1]

Controversy continued as the "Anaconda" music video shattered records, racking up 19.6 million views within its first 24 hours of streaming online. The video caused a stir with its risqué visuals that showed Minaj twerking and dancing suggestively. Drake also made an appearance. Some saw the music video as empowering. "With this video, Nicki Minaj is taking center stage and letting us know that she's in complete control," wrote Rachael Rowsey in Vox.[2] However, others saw it as a ploy for attention. *Today*'s Al Roker called it "vile," adding, "It almost seems like Nicki Minaj has gotten desperate and needs to do something to get her crown back."[3] Minaj didn't seem interested in engaging in conversation about the video. "I don't know what there is to really talk about," she told *GQ*. "I'm being serious. I just see the video as being a normal video."[4]

"I have a whole new level of respect for [Minaj] because of that record."[5]

–Sir Mix-A-Lot on "Anaconda"

Billboard later named "Anaconda" the thirteenth greatest video of the decade. In 2021, it became the first

Minaj's "Anaconda" won praise from Sir Mix-A-Lot, whose hit "Baby Got Back" was heavily sampled in the song.

music video by a solo female rapper to reach one billion views. Listeners may have been divided, but the song and its subsequent music video achieved what Minaj had become an expert at—making people take notice.

LEAVING A MARK

In December 2014, Minaj released *The Pinkprint*, her third studio album. Minaj was a co-executive producer of the

WAX FIGURE

In 2015, Madame Tussauds Wax Museum in Las Vegas created a wax replica of Minaj. The wax figure showed Minaj posed on all fours in an outfit from the jungle-themed "Anaconda" music video. Minaj called the figure "iconic," but many fans thought the replica did not look like the rapper. The wax figure got social media buzzing again when it made its European debut in Germany in 2020.

album. *The Pinkprint*'s title played off Jay-Z's 2001 album *The Blueprint*, which in turn had taken its name from Boogie Down Productions' 1989 album *Ghetto Music: The Blueprint of Hip Hop*. *The Pinkprint*'s tracks included "Only," featuring Drake, Lil Wayne, and Chris Brown, as well as "Get on Your Knees" with

Longtime friends and collaborators, Minaj and Drake shared a stage at a festival in New Jersey in 2014.

Ariana Grande. *The Pinkprint* debuted at Number 2 on the *Billboard* 200, eventually going double platinum. Minaj set out on the *Pinkprint* tour from March to August 2015 to promote the new release.

Critics gave the album high marks, praising it for a more personal tone than Minaj's previous work. In one track, Minaj referenced having an abortion when she was a teenager. In another, she talked about dealing with her cousin's murder. Many listeners found Minaj's vulnerability refreshing. NPR's Kim Osorio called the album "a career-defining moment," adding, "Here the . . . queen offers the most honest, introspective version of the real person who exists underneath the wigs, the makeup, and the red-carpet wardrobes."[6]

NAZI IMAGERY

In 2014, viewers criticized Minaj for having Nazi-inspired imagery in her lyric music video for the song "Only." The video showed images of rallies, gas masks, armbands, and flags reminiscent of Nazi Germany, with Young Money logos in place of Nazi symbols. The Anti-Defamation League condemned the video, calling it offensive and insensitive to Holocaust survivors. While Minaj apologized, the video's director did not apologize for the work.

Minaj took home an American Music Award for *The Pinkprint* in 2015.

THE QUEEN AT WORK

Throughout 2014, Minaj continued promoting her album while appearing on tracks of other artists, including Young Money, Juicy J, August Alsina, Usher, Young Thug, and Wiz Khalifa. She made her third appearance on *Saturday Night Live* as a musical guest, performing "Bed of Lies" with singer Skylar Grey and a medley of "Only" and "All Things Go."

It seemed as though Minaj had finally hit her stride in pursuit of her full potential of being a hip-hop great. *Vogue*'s Alex Frank dubbed 2015 "The Year of Nicki Minaj," writing that "a cooler, smarter, more fearless, and ultimately, more beloved Minaj" had emerged.[7]

THE 48-HOUR POP WAR

In July 2015, MTV's VMAs announced that year's nominations. Minaj had tracks nominated in four categories: "Anaconda" for both Best Female Video and Best Hip-Hop Video, "Bang Bang" for Best Collaboration, and David Guetta's "Hey Mama" for Song of the Summer. However, Minaj took issue with the fact that "Anaconda" was not nominated in the Video of the Year category.

She vented her frustration on social media over what she believed was a snub. In a series of

MEEK MILL

In 2015, Minaj's relationship with rapper Meek Mill often appeared in tabloids and on gossip sites that referred to the duo as a hip-hop power couple. However, not everyone was pleased about the relationship, with Minaj's longtime friend Drake publicly criticizing Meek Mill. The feud between Drake and Meek Mill continued to intensify, with each of them writing diss tracks about the other. In January 2017, Minaj confirmed she and Meek Mill had broken up.

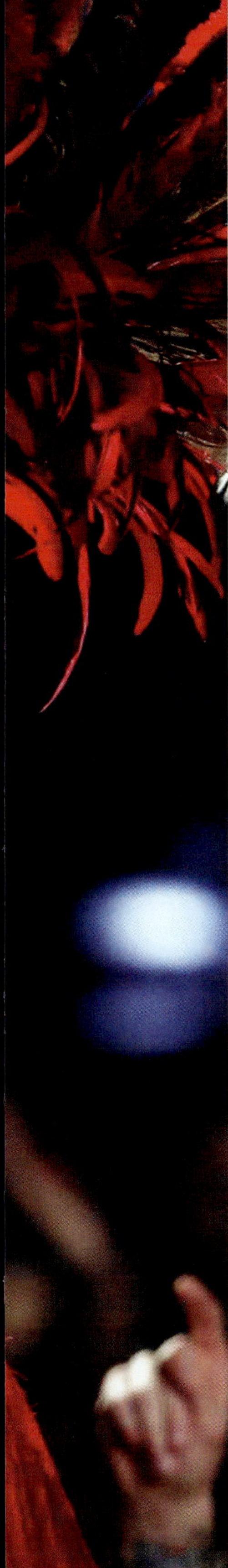

A brief war of words between Minaj and Taylor Swift ended by the time the pair took the stage at the VMAs in 2015.

widely shared tweets, she pointed out that "Anaconda" had a large cultural impact and questioned the role of bias in the music industry. "If I was a different 'kind' of artist, Anaconda would be nominated for best choreo and vid of the year as well," Minaj wrote. "If your video celebrates women with very slim bodies, you will be nominated for vid of the year."[8]

From there, what *Billboard* called "The 48-Hour Pop War" began. Taylor Swift, who led the VMAs in nominations, saw Minaj's tweets as a personal attack and responded that Minaj shouldn't pit women against one another. Meanwhile, other celebrities such as Bruno Mars and Katy Perry jumped into the Twitter conversation with their own thoughts. As a result of all the attention, the terms "Anaconda" and "Nicki" began trending online. After Swift and Minaj reconciled onstage at the VMAs, the dustup seemed to be settled. They performed together at the awards show, with Minaj winning Best Hip-Hop Video for "Anaconda." Swift was the top award winner, taking home four VMAs.

While some criticized Minaj for calling out the awards on social media, some people saw truth in her statements. The situation spurred conversations about institutional racism in the music industry. For instance, *Marie Claire* magazine pointed out that all the 2015 Grammy nominees for Best New Artist and Record of the Year were white, as were most music company executives. There also seemed to be a double standard in how female artists of different races were treated. *Marie Claire* stated that when white women gave controversial performances or adopted Black culture, they were often given praise and awards, but women

MEME-ING MILEY

A few days before the 2015 VMAs, pop star Miley Cyrus waded into the social media fray during an interview with the *New York Times*. Cyrus called Minaj "not too kind" and criticized her for giving the media gossip material. Minaj addressed Cyrus while accepting her award at the VMAs. "And now, back to this [woman] that had a lot to say about me the other day in the press," she said. "Miley, what's good?" Her last line quickly became a meme. MTV described it as "one of pop culture's standout moments of 2015."[9]

of color who attracted controversy were punished. As conversations continued, fans began to notice that Minaj was using her voice in new ways—by speaking up.

SPEAKING UP

Chapter SEVEN

Minaj showed she wasn't afraid to voice her opinions both inside and outside the music studio. In a December 2015 *Billboard* magazine interview, she criticized the War on Drugs and mass incarceration in the United States, which disproportionately affected Black people. She also voiced her support for Black Lives Matter, a movement that had begun in 2013 to protest violence and police brutality against Black people.

Minaj continued incorporating references to current events into her rap verses. A few weeks after real estate mogul Donald Trump won the 2016 US presidential election, Minaj addressed him in her single "Black Barbies," referring to his stance on restricting immigration. She created the track in collaboration with producer Mike Will Made It. "Black Barbies" was a remix of the 2016 track "Black Beatles" by Rae Sremmurd, a rap duo made up of brothers Slim Jxmmi and Swae Lee. Rae Sremmurd's original song featured Gucci Mane. In Minaj's version, she rapped, "Island girl, Donald Trump want me go home."[1]

Minaj has spoken out about issues that are important to her while still pushing her career to new areas.

In January 2017, Minaj tweeted to oppose Trump's ban on immigrants from seven predominantly Muslim countries. "The most harmful thing you could ever take away from another human being is hope," she wrote, adding, "#ProudImmigrant #Grateful #TaxPayerButICantVote #America."[2]

SANDRA BLAND

Minaj has cited the 2015 case of Sandra Bland as striking a personal chord. Bland was a 28-year-old Black woman in Texas who was arrested after a traffic stop and later died by apparent suicide in police custody. Bland's case spurred widespread protests against police brutality. It also sparked the first use of the hashtag #SayHerName, which was later used by activists to call attention to Black female victims of police brutality and anti-Black violence. "This could have been me," Minaj told *Billboard*. "I'm a sassy woman. I may have given a little bit of attitude to a police officer. I could have never come home."[3]

REACHING FOR THE CROWN

Minaj continued making her mark in the hip-hop industry throughout 2016. At the 58th Grammys, she was nominated for three awards: Best Album (*The Pinkprint*), Best Rap Performance ("Truffle Butter," featuring Drake and Lil Wayne), and Best Rap/Sung Collaboration ("Only," featuring Drake, Lil Wayne, and Chris Brown). She lost in each category to rapper Kendrick Lamar, who led the awards in both nominations and wins with 11 and five, respectively.

In 2016, Minaj appeared on *Time* magazine's annual list of the 100 most influential people, which included world leaders, doctors, entrepreneurs, athletes, and artists. Minaj was listed in the "Icon" category. In her magazine profile, Minaj's mentor and collaborator Lil Wayne described the moment when he discovered her a decade earlier on Fendi's street DVD. "When I heard the first two and four bars, it wasn't even about her rapping better than any female rapper," he wrote. "It was about, man, she's rapping better than other rappers—period."[4]

"Minaj has become expert at modeling the ways that women can wield power in the industry. But she has also drawn attention to the ways in which power can be embodied by a woman standing up for herself and speaking her own mind."[5]

—*Music journalist Vanessa Grigoriadis,* New York Times

Minaj continued having success in other areas, including film. She appeared in *Barbershop: The Next Cut*, the third installment of the comedic *Barbershop* film franchise. She played a hairdresser named Draya, acting within an ensemble cast that included Ice Cube, Cedric the Entertainer, Regina Hall, Eve, and other well-known

Minaj's big-screen appearance in the *Barbershop* franchise was well received by critics and fans.

actors. The film received positive reviews, and Minaj was nominated for a Teen Choice Award for her role.

To the delight of her Barbies, Minaj continued releasing new music. In 2016, she featured on Ariana Grande's hit single "Side to Side." The reggae-inspired

dance song went to Number 1 on *Billboard*'s Pop Songs chart, making it Minaj's first time topping the pop charts. Later that year, Minaj and Grande performed "Side to Side" onstage at the MTV Video Music Awards.

MET GALAS

Minaj has made statements with her wardrobe at the annual Met Gala, a fundraiser for New York City's Metropolitan Museum of Art. Each year, the gala has a theme that attendees interpret through creative outfit choices. In 2019, Minaj wore a pink high-to-low dress for the "Camp" theme. In 2018, she wore a red gown with a black headdress for the "Heavenly Bodies" theme. At the 2017 gala, Minaj wore a striking gown with a kimono top, red-and-black coloring, and a long train.

HITTING MILESTONES

Minaj hit a major milestone in March 2017 when the announcement came that she had the most career *Billboard* Hot 100 entries by a female solo artist, with 76. The record-breaking achievement came with the simultaneous release of her tracks "No Frauds," "Changed It," and "Regret in Your Tears." The decades-old record of 73 songs had been held by another "queen"—Aretha Franklin, who was known as the Queen of Soul. In June, Minaj announced that she had become the most awarded female rapper in history with her recent award from the American Society of Composers, Authors and Publishers, surpassing Missy Elliott's 189 awards.

In 2017, Minaj was featured on tracks such as Jason Derulo's single "Swalla," Migos's "Motor Sport," and Yo Gotti's "Rake It Up." In March, she signed a modeling

Minaj continued to turn heads in the fashion world in 2017, including with her dress at the 2017 Met Gala in New York City.

contract with Wilhelmina Models. In May, she featured on Katy Perry's "Swish Swish." Joe Lynch of *Billboard* called her verse a highlight of the basketball-themed song.

In looking back at her career thus far, Minaj said she was appreciative for the challenges she had overcome. "I kind of love that I've had to go through so many hurdles to get where I am because I feel like I deserve it," she told Roxane Gay in the *New York Times Style* magazine.

I had so much going against me in the beginning: being Black, being a woman, being a female rapper. No matter how many times I get on a track with everyone's favorite MC and hold my own, the culture never seems to want to give me my props as an MC, as a lyricist, as a writer. I got to prove myself a hundred times, whereas the guys that came in around the same time as I did, they were given the titles so much quicker without anybody second-guessing.[6]

Although Minaj had a successful year in 2017, some people questioned whether she had lost her touch. Her recent tracks weren't smash hits, and some critics thought she was getting bogged down by industry drama and her alleged feuds. "Minaj's recent collaborations failed to stick both on the

REMY'S RAP

In February 2017, female rapper Remy Ma released the seven-minute track "Shether," an explicit diss track directed at Minaj. At the 2017 Summer Jam concert, Remy Ma performed "Shether" with photos of Minaj displayed on the stage. The two had exchanged barbs in their rap songs for more than a decade. In the opinion of Kathy Iandoli in *Billboard*, the feud was a positive development as it showed that women rappers were engaging in a classic part of hip-hop culture.

charts and in people's minds," noted Bianca Gracie in *Billboard* in 2018.[7] Controversial media personalities Joe Budden and Charlamagne Tha God even went so far as to name her one of the year's "trash artists." Budden stated that Minaj's recent singles hadn't been successful and that she posted too much about her own accolades on social media. "Nicki, I know you're watching this. You watch everything," said Budden. "You cannot have 90,000,000 Instagram followers and put out three records and none of them catch."[8] At the end of the year, Minaj went silent on her social media accounts, leaving her passionate Barbz concerned. They wondered what their queen was up to.

PAYING IT FORWARD

In 2017, Chicago college student Pedro Velazquez received a shock when Minaj paid a portion of his tuition. The gift came after Velazquez tweeted at the rapper following her offer to help fans with tuition and loans. Velazquez told the *Chicago Tribune* that he had come to the United States from Mexico as a young child and was working to put himself through college.

Oscar de
Renta

Chapter EIGHT

HOLDING ON TO THE THRONE

In spring 2018, Minaj began promoting her upcoming album, *Queen*. On April 12, the tenth anniversary of her 2008 mixtape *Sucka Free*, she released two singles: "Barbie Tingz" and "Chun-Li." Both tracks had critics and listeners eager for more, with Minaj earning praise for returning to her gritty rap roots and take-no-prisoners delivery. "Nicki Minaj is finally back—and she's here with a vengeance," wrote Bianca Gracie in *Billboard*.[1]

"Chun-Li" was named after a character in the video game *Street Fighter II*. The song's success led to Minaj earning her first solo Top 10 track on the *Billboard* Hot 100 in four years. In May, she released the official "Chun-Li" video. It went on to win Best Hip-Hop Video at the VMAs. She appeared on *Saturday Night Live* to perform "Chun-Li" as well as a song with rapper Playboi Carti.

A heavier focus on her rap skills drew praise for Minaj's work in 2018.

> **"I'm excited that people use the word 'revive' in association with me and female MCs. I never thought I would be such an instrumental part of anything. . . . But of course, it's like, the best thing to hear because not only am I doing this for me but I'm doing it for so many other girls."[3]**
>
> ***—Nicki Minaj***

The song's lyrics, as well as Minaj's alter ego and representation of Asian cultures, were seen as problematic by some listeners and critics. They accused her of inappropriate use in the video of the customs and dress of other cultures, known as cultural appropriation. They were concerned that Minaj was reducing individual cultures to harmful stereotypes and leading others to do the same.

"Chun-Li" inspired a trending social media activity called the #ChunLiChallenge in which users filmed themselves lip-syncing to the song. Many users filmed themselves in stereotypical East Asian hairstyles or used chopsticks as props, a trend that some viewed as racist. "The bottom line? People should know better by now," wrote David Yi in *Teen Vogue*, adding, "It speaks to a larger issue about how social media commodifies groups and cultural identities."[2]

"Chun-Li" was a major hit, but it was also criticized for cultural appropriation.

A ROYAL ALBUM

In August 2018, Minaj released *Queen* as her fourth studio album, featuring guests Ariana Grande, Eminem, Foxy Brown, Future, and others. Listeners noticed that *Queen* showed a clear return to Minaj's hip-hop roots, with its tracks the most rap-focused of her four albums to date. The album earned positive marks from critics, who pointed out that Minaj out-rapped her guests and showed skill on difficult tracks—even if the songs themselves didn't always live up to expectations. "Nicki hasn't been able to maintain the lyrical 'Monster' she rode in on," wrote Ben Carter of the website CentralSauce, referencing Minaj's iconic 2010 guest verse. "Despite that, *Queen* is a firm acknowledgement of the importance and purity of female rap." He cited the track "Barbie Dreams" as evidence of "a lyrical Goliath finally getting back in the ring."[4]

Queen debuted at Number 2 on the *Billboard* 200. Despite its high ranking, the album did not meet sales expectations. As usual, the most intense pressure on the album's success came from Minaj herself. She was not pleased to have *Queen* sitting in second place to rapper Travis Scott's *Astroworld*. She vented her frustrations on the

QUEEN RADIO

To help promote her *Queen* album, Minaj launched her own radio show in August 2018, called *Queen Radio*, on the Beats 1 station, which was later renamed Apple Music 1. The show quickly became one of the station's most popular programs, with Minaj offering her unfiltered takes on a wide range of topics. "People talk about me all the time and lie about me," Minaj told BET. "It's not fair, and it's not happening anymore. Now with *Queen Radio* . . . I got something to say, too."[5] Minaj selected music playlists, chatted with Barbz, called out her haters, and welcomed surprise guests. "She plays her own music, gets distracted by her phone, shouts, and intimidates guests—it's no wonder why the rapper's Beats 1 show is such fun," wrote Issy Sampson in the *Guardian*, calling the show "deliciously chaotic."[6]

second-place performance by calling out streaming platforms, music charts, and industry executives, as well as Scott and his girlfriend, Kylie Jenner. Some criticized Minaj for blaming others, with Vulture's Dee Lockett writing that she had spun a "tangled web rooted in conspiracy."[7] However, Minaj held that she was simply standing up for herself.

Minaj and Ariana Grande, *left*, have collaborated multiple times.

TAKING TRAVIS TO TASK

Minaj was not pleased that Travis Scott scored the top place on the charts the week of her *Queen* album release—and she was ready to vent about it on social media, talk shows, and her own radio show. Minaj believed that Scott reached Number 1 unfairly by selling merchandise bundles and using the massive popularity of his girlfriend Kylie Jenner to promote the album. She also accused media outlets, her record label, and streaming services for sabotaging her sales.

FEELING THE HEAT

Meanwhile, Minaj was receiving backlash for overblown responses to criticism. She rallied her Barbz to gang up on naysayers, resulting in accusations of cyberbullying. In June, Minaj and Barbz targeted *New York Times* writer Wanna Thompson after Thompson tweeted a criticism of Minaj. When Bryan Rolli, a contributor to *Forbes*, criticized the rollout of Minaj's *Queen* album, outraged fans began an online campaign against him, which included petitions to have him fired.

Meanwhile, the hip-hop landscape was changing as a growing number of female rappers gained success, including Megan Thee Stallion, Saweetie, and Cardi B. Writing for NPR, Sowmya Krishnamurthy pointed out that though Minaj had paved the way for a new era of female rap, it was likely bittersweet for her to see the new crop of rappers having an easier time. "Despite her success, her kingdom isn't impenetrable," wrote Krishnamurthy. "There's challengers coming for her neck . . . and her *Queen* album wasn't the success she had hoped for. But she isn't abdicating without a fight."[8]

AN ARMY OF BARBZ

When Wanna Thompson—a self-described Minaj fan—tweeted mild criticism about the rapper, she never expected that millions of people would see the comment. "The Nicki Minaj stans—or superfans—attacked," wrote Joe Coscarelli in the *New York Times*.[9] After the fuming Barbz brought the tweet to her attention, Minaj entered the conversation and sent Thompson insulting direct messages. Thompson reported receiving thousands of hateful messages and even death threats on her social media accounts and cell phone. The incident spurred conversations about cyberbullying and how fans and celebrities interact with one another.

RETIRING FROM MUSIC

In June 2019, Minaj teamed up with rapper Trina on "BAPS," a single from Trina's album *The One*. In August, Minaj appeared with singer Ty Dolla $ign on Megan Thee Stallion's hit "Hot Girl Summer," named for the popular phrase Megan Thee Stallion had coined. *Billboard* called Minaj's guest verse, in which she displayed alternating voices and clever lyrics, the highlight of the song.

A new generation of female hip-hop artists, which included Cardi B, *center*, emerged as Minaj's career entered its second decade.

In September 2019, Minaj shocked fans when she announced on Twitter that she was retiring from music. "I've decided to retire & have my family," she wrote. "I know you guys are happy now." The announcement left some fans confused—and others skeptical. "There is the sneaking suspicion Minaj might be pulling the biggest troll of 2019," wrote Andre Wheeler in the *Guardian*. "But there's an even worse fear: she's telling the truth."[10]

It seemed as though Minaj was following through on her statement to focus on her personal life. On October 21, 2019, Minaj married 42-year-old Kenneth "Zoo" Petty, whom she had known since growing up in New York. She had confirmed their relationship the previous year on social media. Media outlets reported widely on his past criminal history, as he was a registered sex offender and had served prison time for first-degree manslaughter. In response to the backlash on Petty's past, Minaj wrote on Twitter: "Y'all can't run my life. Y'all can't even run y'all own life."[11]

> **"Some days I'm super strong; some days I'm super insecure. But I don't really identify with any particular label. I just speak my truth and if people like it, they like it, and if they bash it, they bash it."[13]**
>
> ***–Nicki Minaj***

In December 2019, Minaj clarified her retirement announcement in an interview with *Billboard*, saying she didn't think she could ever remove herself completely from her music and fans. However, she didn't want to box herself in. "I do believe it is important to become a woman outside of the magnifying glass," she said. "I have to make sure that I'm well-rounded as a human being."[12]

Chapter NINE

THE NEXT ERA

The year 2020 came with highs and lows. In late January, 37-year-old Minaj returned to social media after a three-month break. In February, she told the audience at a live interview event that she shouldn't have made the announcement of retiring from music. She said she deleted her social media from her phone to keep herself from making hasty posts in the future. The following week, she released a new track called "Yikes," teased an eventual fifth album, and introduced a new alter ego named "Queen Sleaze." According to Minaj, the new persona was "more calm but way deadlier" than her existing alter egos.[1] Later in 2020, Minaj made history as the richest woman in rap music, with an estimated net worth of $100 million.

Meanwhile, the world was changing. The COVID-19 pandemic was sweeping the globe, causing an estimated 75 million cases and 1.6 million deaths worldwide by the end of 2020.[2] The pandemic changed the music industry,

Minaj's retirement proved to be short-lived, and she returned to the public eye within a few months.

Theaters and music venues around the world shut down during the worst of the COVID-19 pandemic.

as virtually all in-person tours and live performances were canceled.

In the United States, people also were grappling with racial injustice and civil unrest. The May 2020 death of George Floyd, a Black man, in police custody in Minneapolis, Minnesota, led to widespread protests over police brutality, spurring debates on racism and policing. Minneapolis police officer Derek Chauvin would later be convicted of murder in Floyd's death. Minaj spoke out about the incident and called for the police officers involved to be brought to justice. "Let your voice be heard," she wrote on Instagram. "Be angry. White people have been using violence against us since the beginning of time."[3] She expressed support for the Black Lives Matter movement and posted links to donate to various social justice organizations.

In May 2020, Minaj hit a career milestone—she reached Number 1 on the *Billboard* Hot 100 for the first time when she was featured on the remix of singer-rapper Doja Cat's song "Say So." The song was Minaj's 109th time on the chart. The following month, Minaj hit

Minaj has collaborated with up-and-coming rappers, such as Doja Cat.

Number 1 on the Hot 100 again, this time as the guest on the song "Trollz" by 6ix9ine. She received backlash for the collaboration with the controversial Brooklyn-born rapper, who has been referred to by Rolling Stone as a "hip-hop supervillain" for his criminal background.[4] Even so, it seemed as though the Queen were back with a vengeance. Minaj became the second female rapper in history to debut in the top slot, the first being Lauryn Hill in 1998. On Twitter, Minaj posted, "No words yet. All I can muster up is the 'I love you'. Gimme a sec," along with rainbow and unicorn emojis.[5] By the end of the year, her popularity made her Spotify's most-streamed artist of 2020.

FAMILY AND LEGAL ISSUES

Minaj's family life was also in the headlines. On September 30, 2020, Minaj and her husband welcomed a son whose name they did not reveal publicly. "Becoming a mom is by far the most fulfilling job I've ever taken on," she posted on social media.[6] Shocking news came in February 2021 when Minaj's father was killed in a hit-and-run accident in Mineola, New York, while crossing the street. The driver was arrested a few days later after leaving the scene of the accident without calling for help.

Minaj did not discuss his death until a few months later, when she called it "the most devastating loss of my life."[7] Minaj's mother, Carol, filed a $150 million lawsuit against the driver.

In January 2021, singer-songwriter Tracy Chapman won a case against Minaj for using her work without permission. Minaj had included the melody and lyrics of Chapman's 1988 song "Baby Can I Hold You" on her 2018 song "Sorry," featuring rapper Nas. As a result of the ruling, Minaj paid Chapman $450,000.[8]

TRACY CHAPMAN SUES

In 2018, Tracy Chapman sued Minaj for using her work without permission on "Sorry." According to Chapman, her team rejected Minaj's request to use her song "Baby Can I Hold You." However, Chapman believed Minaj had already recorded the song, as Minaj was going to use it on the *Queen* album set to be released the following month. Minaj also tweeted—but then deleted—that she had accidentally used Chapman's song, polling her followers about whether she should delay the album release or pull the song. She also tweeted Chapman asking her to approve the song's use. "Sorry" was not included on the *Queen* album. However, the song leaked on the radio and online.

RETURN OF THE QUEEN

In 2021, Minaj took another break from social media. Through the first four months of the year, she didn't release any new music. On Monday, May 10, Minaj came back online, posting photos of herself with the caption "Friday." The post got fans buzzing with anticipation over new music. On Friday, May 14, Minaj made several surprise announcements. During an Instagram Live discussion with her friend Drake, she talked about her return to music. "We miss the bars, we miss the excitement that you bring," he told her.[9] Minaj reported that she was working on her fifth album. There was also an HBO Max documentary series about her in the works.

During the discussion, Minaj announced that she was rereleasing her 2009 mixtape, *Beam Me Up Scotty*, and that it would be available immediately. The release had 23 tracks total, including three new songs. Drake and Lil Wayne guested on a new track, "Seeing Green." Fans and critics gave the rerelease a warm reception,

CLASS OF YOUNG MONEY

Upon the rerelease of *Beam Me Up Scotty*, Minaj tweeted a graphic titled "Class of Young Money" showing yearbook-style headshots of herself, Lil Wayne, and Drake. Each had a second photo of an alternate persona: Barbie, Weezy, and Drizzy, respectively. Answering fan questions, Minaj wrote that Lil Wayne and Drake had "washed," or bested, her with their verses on her new song "Seeing Green." She posted, "I'm woman enough to admit when I've been washed on a track by the Greats and it's ok #Barbz I've washed them b4 . . . I was still a lil rusty."[10]

Minaj's huge fan base has followed many twists and turns in her career, and in 2021 fans were excited to see what she would do next.

appreciating the nostalgia of the album as well as its new additions.

Minaj told fans that her break had been beneficial for her mental health. According to Minaj, she was able to spend time with her son, write, and work on other projects. "It's so important to always go back to basics for me," she wrote in an open letter on her website. "This world of smoke & mirrors can blind you. Be careful."[11]

As it had been three years since her last studio album, the Barbz could not wait for Minaj's next album to drop. Fans took to the internet to speculate about the upcoming album, referring to it as "NM5." They pieced together information about the title and tracks from Minaj's various tweets, lyrics, and interviews from the past few years. By mid-2021, no release date had been announced.

HIP-HOP LEGACY

The hip-hop landscape has changed significantly since Minaj burst onto the scene in the first decade of the millennium—and many of those changes are due to Minaj herself. According to documentary filmmaker Ava Duvernay, there were upwards of 40 female rappers signed to major labels in the "golden era of hip-hop" in the late 1980s to early 1990s. By 2010, the number had dwindled to three.

"I love that people never know what Nicki they are going to get on a particular song. I like bringing out a different side. I think that's what rappers should do. I pride myself on always having a magical moment."[12]

–Nicki Minaj

Minaj shook up the male-dominated industry with her chameleonlike ability to switch personae and styles, offering witty lyrics, outspoken opinions, and unwavering confidence. "She quite simply broadened the definition of hip-hop, making it more joyful, energetic, and robust," wrote Roxane Gay in the *New York Times Style* magazine.[13] Critics took aim at her blend of pop and rap styles, her unapologetic sexuality, and her fervent fan base. She courted controversy with performances, social media callouts, alter egos, and feuds. Her defenders have attributed some criticisms to sexist double standards, as Minaj seemed to have to play by different rules than her male counterparts. Still, she wasn't content to be boxed in, and she was ready to prove herself again and again as a worthy candidate to be named the greatest of all time.

Minaj's legacy is perhaps best seen in the new crop of successful female rappers for whom she paved the way. Despite

A LONG MEMORY

When the 2021 Grammy nominees were announced, Minaj used the opportunity to remind her followers that she had been snubbed back in 2012. "Never forget the Grammys didn't give me my best new artist award when I had 7 songs simultaneously charting on Billboard & bigger first week than any female rapper in the last decade—went on to inspire a generation," she wrote. "They gave it to the white man Bon Iver. #PinkFriday."[14] As of 2021, Minaj had been nominated for ten Grammys but had not yet won.

her lasting influence, some music journalists predicted that her time at the top was over. In 2021, *Rolling Stone*'s Mankaprr Conteh wrote that the female rappers following

The Trap Music Museum in Atlanta, Georgia, features an exhibit on Minaj, demonstrating the legacy she has already built.

in Minaj's footsteps were now outshining her, adding that rap music "could be headed to a place where Nicki Minaj may become obsolete."[15] *Nylon*'s Demicia Inman pointed out that the move from the top spot was natural. Many newcomer rappers, both male and female, who credited Minaj as inspiration were now superstars themselves. Inman wrote, "Her solo spot at the top is gone, but only for the better."[16]

"Looking back now, I love that I was pushed to reinvent myself, because when I sit back and I really look, I need hip-hop, and hip-hop needs me."[17]

—Nicki Minaj

With best-selling records, armfuls of awards, and a brand that spanned music, fashion, radio, film, television, and more, there was no doubt Minaj had succeeded in building an empire. Fans and critics alike waited to see whether she would fight to keep her crown, relinquish it to the new generation, or do something completely new. After more than a decade of reigning supreme as a cultural icon, one thing was certain—the Queen never did the expected.

TIMELINE

1982

On December 8, Onika Tanya Maraj is born in Port of Spain, Trinidad and Tobago.

2007

Minaj is discovered on Myspace by Dirty Money Entertainment CEO Big Fendi and soon catches the attention of Lil Wayne.

Minaj releases the mixtape *Playtime Is Over*.

2008

Minaj releases the mixtape *Sucka Free*.

2009

Minaj releases the mixtape *Beam Me Up Scotty*.

In August, Minaj becomes the first female artist to sign to Lil Wayne's Young Money Entertainment label.

2010

Minaj gains widespread acclaim for her guest verse on Kanye West's "Monster" track.

In November, Minaj releases her first studio album, *Pink Friday*.

2011

In April, Minaj releases her single "Super Bass," which becomes the highest-charting rap song by a female solo artist since 2002.

2012

In February, Minaj releases the single "Starships."

In April, Minaj releases her second studio album, *Pink Friday: Roman Reloaded*.

2014

In August, Minaj releases the single "Anaconda."

In December, Minaj releases her third studio album, *The Pinkprint*.

2016

Minaj appears on *Time* magazine's list of the 100 most influential people.

2018

In August, Minaj releases her fourth studio album, *Queen*.

2019

On October 21, Minaj marries Kenneth Petty.

2020

In May, Minaj reaches Number 1 on the *Billboard* Hot 100 for the first time with her feature on Doja Cat's "Say So."

On September 30, Minaj gives birth to a son with husband Petty.

2021

In February, Minaj's father, Robert, is killed in a hit-and-run accident.

In May, Minaj rereleases her mixtape *Beam Me Up Scotty* with additional tracks.

ESSENTIAL FACTS

FULL NAME

Onika Tanya Maraj-Petty

DATE OF BIRTH

December 8, 1982

PLACE OF BIRTH

Saint James, Port of Spain, Trinidad and Tobago

PARENTS

Carol and Robert Maraj

EDUCATION

Fiorello H. LaGuardia High School, New York City

CAREER HIGHLIGHTS

After getting her start with Lil Wayne's record label, Minaj proved herself a force to be reckoned with on high-profile collaborations, including a standout verse on Kanye West's 2010 track "Monster." Her debut album's first single, the pop crossover smash "Super Bass," introduced her to mainstream audiences and made her into a household name. Other hit singles include "Starships" (2012), "Anaconda" (2014), and "Chun-Li" (2018). Minaj has also done collaborations with Ariana Grande, Britney Spears, Eminem, Jessie J, Drake, Trey Songz, David Guetta, and others. In 2017, she surpassed Aretha Franklin's record for more *Billboard* Top 100 hits than any other female artist in history. In 2020, Minaj reached Number 1 on the Hot 100 chart for the first and second time in her career through her features on Doja Cat's "Say So" and 6ix9ine's "Trollz," respectively.

ALBUMS

Pink Friday (2010); *Pink Friday: Roman Reloaded* (2012); *The Pinkprint* (2014); *Queen* (2018)

CONTRIBUTION TO HIP-HOP

Minaj disrupted the hip-hop industry, which had historically been dominated by male rappers. She brought to her work an assortment of personae and styles, bold performances, and an unshakable confidence. Her most lasting legacy may be ushering in the modern era of successful female rappers. She has become a cultural icon and has influenced both female and male musical artists.

CONFLICTS

Minaj faced conflicts early in life because of her father's drug addiction and abuse. As she grew in her career, many conflicts stemmed from expectations within the male-dominated hip-hop industry. The media has often reported on Minaj's conflicts with other artists, including Lil' Kim, Cardi B, and Remy Ma. Her sexually suggestive videos and lyrics have sparked debate, with supporters calling them empowering and detractors calling them degrading. Minaj has received criticism for appropriating Asian cultures in lyrics, videos, and her Chun-Li persona.

QUOTE

"I kind of love that I've had to go through so many hurdles to get where I am because I feel like I deserve it."

—Nicki Minaj

GLOSSARY

ABORTION

The purposeful ending of a pregnancy.

BAR

A section of music that has a specific number of beats.

BOROUGH

In New York City, one of the five major areas that make up the city: the Bronx, Brooklyn, Manhattan, Queens, and Staten Island.

COMMODIFY

To turn into something that can be bought or sold.

ENSEMBLE CAST

A group of actors who have the same importance and screen time within a movie, TV show, or play.

EXORCISM

The act of trying to get rid of an evil spirit.

FEMINIST

Believing in equality of the sexes; supporting women's rights.

FREESTYLE

Improvisational.

GOLIATH

A powerful, giant warrior.

INSTITUTIONAL

Having to do with an established law or practice in a society.

MASS INCARCERATION

Imprisonment of a large number of people.

MC

A person who speaks over a beat; interchangeable with "rapper."

SAMPLE

A piece of recorded music used by DJs or producers to make new music.

SEXIST

Discriminating based on sex, often against women.

STEREOTYPE

A widely held but oversimplified idea about a particular type of person or thing.

TRENDING

Becoming popular or widely mentioned.

TWERKING

Dancing by squatting and thrusting the hips.

UNDOCUMENTED IMMIGRANT

A foreign-born person who lives in a country without legal documentation or government authorization.

ADDITIONAL RESOURCES

SELECTED BIBLIOGRAPHY

Carter, Ben. "'Queen' of Rap: Nicki Minaj Defends Her Throne with the Most Rap of Her Career." *CentralSauce*, 14 Aug. 2018, centralsauce.com. Accessed 29 June 2021.

Greene, Andy. "Nicki Minaj Opens Up on Childhood Abuse, Sexuality." *Rolling Stone*, 1 Dec. 2010, rollingstone.com. Accessed 29 June 2021.

Krishnamurthy, Sowmya. "Nicki Minaj Is the 21st Century's Insatiable Hip-Hop Monarch." *NPR*, 3 Oct. 2018, npr.org. Accessed 29 June 2021.

FURTHER READINGS

Kallen, Stuart A. *Nicki Minaj*. ReferencePoint, 2020.

Llanas, Sheila. *The Women of Hip-Hop*. Abdo, 2018.

Lusted, Marcia Amidon. *Hip-Hop Music*. Abdo, 2018.

ONLINE RESOURCES

Booklinks
NONFICTION NETWORK
FREE! ONLINE NONFICTION RESOURCES

To learn more about Nicki Minaj, please visit **abdobooklinks.com** or scan this QR code. These links are routinely monitored and updated to provide the most current information available.

MORE INFORMATION

For more information on this subject, contact or visit the following organizations:

BILLBOARD
1540 Broadway
New York, NY 10001
billboard.com

Billboard produces a music-focused magazine and website and is known for its music charts that track sales of various genres.

UNIVERSAL HIP HOP MUSEUM
PO Box 6001
Bronx, NY 10451
347-454-2793
info@uhhm.org
uhhm.org

The Universal Hip Hop Museum celebrates and preserves the history of local and global hip-hop music and culture. It offers educational activities and resources for K–12 schools.

UNIVERSAL MUSIC GROUP
2220 Colorado Ave.
Santa Monica, CA 90404
universalmusic.com

Universal Music Group is the parent company of Young Money Entertainment, the record label founded by rapper Lil Wayne, who would become Nicki Minaj's mentor. Minaj's first four albums were released by Young Money.

SOURCE NOTES

CHAPTER 1. DROPPING THE SUPER BASS

1. Tatiana Cirisano. "Songs that Defined the Decade: Nicki Minaj's 'Super Bass.'" *Billboard*, 21 Nov. 2019, billboard.com. Accessed 3 Apr. 2021.

2. Cirisano, "Songs that Defined the Decade."

3. Jason S. Lipshutz. "Nicki Minaj Catches Eyes." *Billboard*, 10 Aug. 2009, billboard.com. Accessed 17 Apr. 2021.

4. Brandon Soderberg. "What Makes Nicki Minaj's Music Fun and Smart." *Spin*, 20 May 2011, spin.com. Accessed 11 Apr. 2021.

5. Dan Weiss. "Nicki Minaj's 13 Best Singing Moments." *Billboard*, 29 Oct. 2016, billboard.com. Accessed 11 Apr. 2021.

6. Kat George. "Why Missy Elliott's Feminist Legacy Is Criminally Underrated." *Dazed*, 22 Jan. 2016, dazeddigital.com. Accessed 19 May 2021.

7. Caryn Ganz. "The Curious Case of Nicki Minaj." *Out*, 12 Sept. 2010, out.com. Accessed 4 Aug. 2021.

CHAPTER 2. FROM TRINIDAD TO NEW YORK

1. Emily Yahr. "Nicki Minaj Said She Had a Horrific Childhood." *Chicago Tribune*, 30 Sept. 2015, chicagotribune.com. Accessed 17 Apr. 2021.

2. Alex Frank. "Newly Single Nicki Minaj on Feminism, Meek Mill, and Rapping at 50." *Vogue*, 12 Feb. 2015, vogue.com. Accessed 2 Jun. 2021.

3. Eva Chen. "Nicki Minaj Speaks Her Mind about Everything." *Teen Vogue*, 13 May 2013, teenvogue.com. Accessed 1 May 2021.

4. "Nicki Minaj." *Republic Records*, n.d., republicrecords.com. Accessed 15 Mar. 2021.

5. Caryn Ganz. "The Curious Case of Nicki Minaj." *Out*, 12 Sept. 2010, out.com. Accessed 4 Aug. 2021.

6. Chen, "Nicki Minaj Speaks Her Mind."

7. Gerrick D. Kennedy. "Nicki Minaj Red-Hot as 'Pink Friday' Lands." *Los Angeles Times*, 26 Nov. 2010, latimes.com. Accessed 8 May 2021.

8. Chen, "Nicki Minaj Speaks Her Mind."

9. Todd Davis. "Nicki Minaj: On the Rise." *RapIndustry*, 20 July 2008, rapindustry.com. Accessed 18 Apr. 2021.

CHAPTER 3. OF MONSTERS AND MIXTAPES

1. "Nicki Minaj Explains Harajuku Barbie." *Def Pen*, 9 Aug. 2009, defpen.com. Accessed 4 Aug. 2021.

2. "XXclusive: Nicki Minaj Signs with Young Money/Universal." *XXL Mag*, 31 Aug. 2009, xxlmag.com. Accessed 30 May 2021.

3. Jason S. Lipshutz. "Nicki Minaj Catches Eyes." *Billboard*, 10 Aug. 2009, billboard.com. Accessed 17 Apr. 2021.

4. Mawuse Ziegbe. "Nicki Minaj's Career Full of Life-Altering Moments." *MTV*, 27 Jan. 2011, mtv.com. Accessed 17 Apr. 2021.

5. Jayson Rodriguez. "Drake, Nicki Minaj Talk Jay-Z and Lil Wayne." *MTV*, 16 Mar. 2010, mtv.com. Accessed 17 Apr. 2021.

6. "Nicki Minaj's 20 Best Features: Staff Picks." *Billboard*, 15 May 2020, billboard.com. Accessed 28 Mar. 2021.

7. Gerrick D. Kennedy. "Nicki Minaj Red-Hot as 'Pink Friday' Lands." *Los Angeles Times*, 26 Nov. 2010, latimes.com. Accessed 8 May 2021.

8. Christopher Weingarten. "The 20 Worst Songs of 2010." *Village Voice*, 14 Dec. 2010, villagevoice.com. Accessed 4 May 2021.

9. Tom Breihan. "Kanye West: 'Monster.'" *Pitchfork*, 7 Sept. 2010, pitchfork.com. Accessed 2 May 2021.

10. "Nicki Minaj's 20 Best Features: Staff Picks."

11. Lizzy Goodman. "Nicki Minaj, the Rapper with a Crush on Meryl Streep." *New York Magazine*, 16 June 2010, nymag.com. Accessed 22 May 2021.

CHAPTER 4. RAP QUEEN OR POP PRINCESS?

1. Mariel Concepcion. "Nicki Minaj: The Billboard Cover Story." *Billboard*, 12 Nov. 2010, billboard.com. Accessed 22 May 2021.

2. Mawuse Ziegbe. "Nicki Minaj's Career Full of Life-Altering Moments." *MTV*, 27 Jan. 2011, mtv.com. Accessed 17 Apr. 2021.

3. Laura M. Holson. "It's Nicki's World." *New York Times*, 7 Jan. 2012, nytimes.com. Accessed 8 May 2021.

4. "The Style Evolution of Nicki Minaj." *Hype Hair*, 2010, hypehair.com. Accessed 18 Apr. 2021.

5. "Nicki Minaj Talks Grammy Performance, Madonna, M.I.A. & 'Starships.'" *The Rap-Up*, 13 Feb. 2012, rap-up.com. Accessed 8 May 2021.

6. Andrew Martin. "Nicki Minaj Responds to Grammy Performance Criticism, Explains Her 'Vision.'" *Prefix Magazine*, 14 Feb. 2012, prefixmag.com. Accessed 31 May 2021.

CHAPTER 5. STARSHIPS ASCENDING

1. "Track Review: Nicki Minaj, 'Starships.'" *Billboard*, 5 Mar. 2012, billboard.com. Accessed 8 May 2021.

2. Jon Caramanica. "A Singular Influence." *New York Times*, 30 Mar. 2012. Accessed 3 Apr. 2021.

3. Matthew Cole. "Review: Nicki Minaj, Pink Friday: Roman Reloaded." *Slant*, 2 Apr. 2012, slant.com. Accessed 8 May 2021.

4. Ben Carter. "'Queen' of Rap: Nicki Minaj Defends Her Throne." *CentralSauce*, 14 Aug. 2018, centralsauce.com. Accessed 8 May 2021.

5. Jody Rosen. "Pink Friday: Roman Reloaded." *Rolling Stone*, 6 Apr. 2012, rollingstone.com. Accessed 8 May 2021.

6. Hannah Miet. "Nicki Minaj Skips Summer Jam." *Atlantic*, 5 June 2012, theatlantic.com. Accessed 17 Apr. 2021.

7. Jon Caramanica. "Nicki Minaj Skips Festival after a DJ's Remarks," *New York Times*, 4 June 2012, nytimes.com. Accessed 8 May 2021.

8. Craig Berman. "Don't Hate! Nicki Minaj Is Awesome on 'American Idol.'" *Today*, 20 Mar. 2013, today.com. Accessed 8 May 2021.

9. Eva Chen. "Nicki Minaj Speaks Her Mind About Everything." *Teen Vogue*, 13 May 2013, teenvogue.com. Accessed 1 May 2021.

10. Maura Johnston. "How Pop Stars Killed 'American Idol.'" *Rolling Stone*, 7 Apr. 2016, rollingstone.com. Accessed 8 May 2021.

11. Joshua Espinoza. "Nicki Minaj on Acting: I Don't Think I'll Ever Do That Again." *Complex*, 17 Aug. 2018, complex.com. Accessed 22 May 2021.

CHAPTER 6. MAKING A PINKPRINT

1. A. J. Delgado. "Nicki Minaj Is Worse for Young Girls' Morals Than Madonna Ever Was." *National Review*, 25 Aug. 2014, nationalreview.com. Accessed 4 Aug. 2021.

2. Rachel Rowsey. "Review: Nicki Minaj Exerts Feminine Power in 'Anaconda.'" *Vox*, 4 Sept. 2014, vox.com. Accessed 22 May 2021.

3. "Al on Nicki Minaj's Racy 'Anaconda' Video: 'It's Just Vile.'" *Today*, 21 Aug. 2014, today.com. Accessed 22 May 2021.

4. Taffy Brodesser-Akner. "Nicki Minaj: Cheeky Genius." *GQ*, 19 Oct. 2014, gq.com. Accessed 13 May 2021.

SOURCE NOTES CONTINUED

5. Danielle Harling. "Nicki Minaj's 'Anaconda' Dubbed New & Improved 'Baby Got Back' by Sir Mix-A-Lot." *HipHopDX*, 12 Aug. 2014, hiphopdx.com. Accessed 9 May 2021.

6. Kim Osario. "On 'The Pinkprint,' Nicki Minaj Speaks the Language of Love." *NPR*, 18 Dec. 2014, npr.com. Accessed 13 May 2021.

7. Alex Frank. "Why 2015 Was the Year of Nicki Minaj." *Vogue*, 29 Dec. 2015, vogue.com. Accessed 2 Jun. 2021.

8. "The Truth about Racism in the Music Industry." *Marie Claire*, 2 Feb. 2016, marieclaire.com. Accessed 13 May 2021.

9. Adam Fleischer. "Nicki Minaj Explains Why She Had to Call Out Miley Cyrus at the VMAs." *MTV*, 7 Oct. 2015, mtv.com. Accessed 11 May 2021.

CHAPTER 7. SPEAKING UP

1. Estelle Tang. "Nicki Minaj Has Something to Say to Donald Trump." *Elle*, 15 Nov. 2016, elle.com. Accessed 17 Apr. 2021.

2. Cavan Sieczkowski. "Nicki Minaj Captures the Agony and Irony of Trump's Immigration Ban." *HuffPost*, 30 Jan. 2017, huffpost.com. Accessed 23 May 2021.

3. "Nicki Minaj Gets Political." *Billboard*, 10 Dec. 2015, billboard.com. Accessed 17 Apr. 2021.

4. Lil Wayne. "Nicki Minaj." *Time*, 21 Apr. 2016, time.com. Accessed 11 Apr. 2021.

5. Vanessa Grigoriadis. "The Passion of Nicki Minaj." *New York Times*, 7 Oct. 2015, nytimes.com. Accessed 1 May 2021.

6. Roxane Gay. "Nicki Minaj, Always in Control." *New York Times*, 16 Oct. 2017, nytimes.com. 2 June 2021.

7. Bianca Gracie. "Nicki Minaj's 'Barbie Tingz' & 'Chun-Li' Are the Return to Form We've Been Waiting For." *Billboard*, 13 Apr. 2018, billboard.com. Accessed 17 May 2021.

8. Jessica McKinney. "Joe Budden on Nicki Minaj: 'She Has Exhibited A Lot of F— Trash.'" *BET*, 27 Dec. 2017, bet.com. Accessed 1 June 2021.

CHAPTER 8. HOLDING ON TO THE THRONE

1. Bianca Gracie. "Nicki Minaj's 'Barbie Tingz' & 'Chun-Li' Are the Return to Form We've Been Waiting For." *Billboard*, 13 Apr. 2018, billboard.com. Accessed 17 May 2021.

2. David Yi. "The Chun Li Challenge Is the Latest Example of Pop Culture Stereotyping Asian Culture." *Teen Vogue*, 27 Apr. 2018, teenvogue.com. Accessed 17 May 2021.

3. Gerrick D. Kennedy. "Nicki Minaj Red-Hot as 'Pink Friday' Lands." *Los Angeles Times*, 26 Nov. 2010, latimes.com. Accessed 8 May 2021.

4. Ben Carter. "'Queen' of Rap: Nicki Minaj Defends Her Throne." *CentralSauce*, 14 Aug. 2018, centralsauce.com. Accessed 4 Aug. 2021.

5. Joshua Espinoza. "Nicki Minaj on Acting: I Don't Think I'll Ever Do That Again." *Complex*, 17 Aug. 2018, complex.com. Accessed 22 May 2021.

6. Issy Sampson. "Beats in the Trap: Nicki Minaj's Queen Show Is Radio's Chaotic, Addictive Monster." *Guardian*, 22 Sept. 2018, theguardian.com. Accessed 2 June 2021.

7. Dee Lockett. "Nicki Minaj's Terrible, Horrible, No Good, Very Bad Week." *Vulture*, 24 Aug. 2018, vulture.com. Accessed 2 June 2021.

8. Sowmya Krishnamurthy. "Nicki Minaj Is the 21st Century's Insatiable Hip-Hop Monarch." *NPR*, 3 Oct. 2018, npr.com. Accessed 28 Mar. 2021.

9. Joe Coscarelli. "How One Tweet about Nicki Minaj Spiraled into Internet Chaos." *New York Times*, 10 July 2018, nytimes.com. Accessed 16 May 2021.

10. Andre Wheeler. "Did We Make Nicki Minaj Retire—or Is She Pulling the Biggest Troll of 2019?" *Guardian*, 5 Sept. 2019, theguardian.com. Accessed 4 May 2021.

11. Michael Saponara. "5 Things to Know About Kenneth Petty." *Billboard*, 12 June 2020, billboard.com. Accessed 23 May 2021.

12. Elise Brisco and Amy Haneline. "Nicki Minaj Is Back! Rapper Rereleases 'Beam Me Up Scotty' Mixtape on Streaming Services with New Songs." *USA Today*, 14 May 2021, usatoday.com. Accessed 4 June 2021.

13. Alex Frank. "Newly Single Nicki Minaj on Feminism, Meek Mill, and Rapping at 50." *Vogue*, 12 Feb. 2015, vogue.com. Accessed 2 June 2021.

CHAPTER 9. THE NEXT ERA

1. Shaad D'Souza. "Nicki Minaj Gives Update on Forthcoming Album, Shares Snippet of New Single." *Fader*, 5 Feb. 2020, thefader.com. Accessed 4 June 2021.

2. "Weekly Epidemiological Update—22 December 2020." *World Health Organization*, 22 Dec. 2020, who.int. Accessed 4 June 2021.

3. Hayden Brooks. "Nicki Minaj Shares Her Outrage over George Floyd's Death: 'Be Angry.'" *iHeart*, 2 June 2020, iheart.com. Accessed 4 Aug. 2021.

4. Stephen Witt. "Tekashi 6ix9ine: The Rise and Fall of a Hip-Hop Supervillain." *Rolling Stone*, 16 Jan. 2019, rollingstone.com. Accessed 2 June 2021.

5. @NICKIMINAJ. "no words yet. All I can muster up is the 'I love you'. Gimme a sec." *Twitter*, 22 June 2020, 12:56 p.m., twitter.com.

6. Elise Brisco and Amy Haneline. "Nicki Minaj Is Back! Rapper Rereleases 'Beam Me Up Scotty' Mixtape on Streaming Services with New Songs." *USA Today*, 14 May 2021, usatoday.com. Accessed 4 June 2021.

7. Elise Brisco. "'Most Devasting Loss of My Life'; Nicki Minaj Writes about Her Father's Death." *USA Today*, 15 May 2021, usatoday.com. Accessed 28 May 2021.

8. Anastasia Tsioulcas. "Tracy Chapman Wins Lawsuit against Nicki Minaj." *NPR*, 8 Jan. 2021, npr.com. Accessed 23 May 2021.

9. Janine Puhak. "Nicki Minaj Re-Releases Monumental 2009 Mixtape *Beam Me Up Scotty*." *People*, 14 May 2021, people.com. Accessed 15 May 2021.

10. Mackenzie Cummings-Grady. "Nicki Minaj Says Drake and Lil Wayne 'Washed' Her on 'Seeing Green.'" *Complex*, 16 May 2021, complex.com. Accessed 3 June 2021.

11. Puhak, "Nicki Minaj Re-Releases Monumental 2009 Mixtape."

12. Alex Frank. "Newly Single Nicki Minaj on Feminism, Meek Mill, and Rapping at 50." *Vogue*, 12 Feb. 2015, vogue.com. Accessed 2 June 2021.

13. Roxane Gay. "Nicki Minaj, Always in Control," *New York Times*, 16 Oct. 2017, nytimes.com. Accessed 2 June 2021.

14. Mike Vulpo. "Nicki Minaj Just Called Out the Grammys 8 Years after Her Best New Artist Snub." *EOnline*, 24 Nov. 2020, eonline.com. Accessed 3 June 2021.

15. Mankaprr Conteh. "Nicki Minaj Revisits a Distant Golden Age with 'Beam Me Up Scotty.'" *Rolling Stone*, 20 May 2021, rollingstone.com. Accessed 31 May 2021.

16. Demicia Inman. "10 Years after 'Pink Friday,' a Look at Nicki Minaj's Enduring Legacy." *Nylon*, 23 Nov. 2020, nylon.com. Accessed 2 June 2021.

17. "Nicki Minaj." *Grammy Awards*, n.d., grammy.com. Accessed 28 Mar. 2021.

INDEX

ABOUT THE AUTHOR

LAURA K. MURRAY

Laura K. Murray has written more than 90 nonfiction books on subjects ranging from music and pop culture to history and science. Her favorite thing about writing books on musical artists is discovering new songs. She lives in Minnesota.